The Ayresome Angel

A Boro football fantasy for those of us
who steadfastly refuse to grow up

John Wilson

Juniper Publishing

First published in Great Britain
by
Juniper Publishing
2007

Typesetting and origination
Norton James Design,
11, Caldey Gardens, Ingleby Barwick
Stockton-on-Tees
TS17 5HW

ISBN 978-0-95465489-3-3

Printed and bound by
Printfine Ltd
Gibraltar Row, King Edward Industrial Estate,
Liverpool
L3 7HJ

Dedication

For those of us, mature in years, who have totally lost the plot with regard to the modern football game and yearn for a time when:

- The only sky was the azure blue above us.

- All matches kicked off at 3pm on Saturday.

- FA Cup draws were on Monday lunchtime and replays the following week.

- 'Uncle' Cliff Mitchell told us exactly what was happening at the club and it wasn't just speculation.

- We were supporters and not customers.

- John O'Rourke gave us a goal and Big John ran a mile to take a penalty.

- There were no radio football phone-ins.

- We stood outside the local newsagent at 5.30pm on a Saturday evening eagerly anticipating the arrival of 'The Sports.'

- Hair was thick and curly brown and not an ever-thinning grey.

- Bede Hall, The Billingham Forum, The Brunswick Bowl, Braid Crescent, Pan's People and Ayresome Park were the centre of the known universe.

Happy days.

Chapter One

It was Christmas Eve, and nine-year-old Jack Hartley had been lying wide-awake for what seemed, to him, an eternity.

The present he was desperately hoping to receive was the latest red Middlesbrough Football Club home shirt, but the ever-growing sense of anticipation was making his stomach churn. So to waste some more time, he got out of bed and opened the curtains.

From his window the headlamps of the nocturnal articulated lorries were clearly visible in the distance, as they pounded their monotonous way across the A19 flyover alongside the Newport Bridge.

To his total surprise he could see, in the soft orange beam of the streetlight outside "The Willows", Union Street, that it was snowing quite heavily. He could never remember it snowing at Christmas before. This was brilliant. If it lay, his dad might even take him sledging in Stewart Park.

Suddenly, there was a noise from downstairs, so he quickly darted back into bed. He presumed it must be his parents placing the presents round the tree. His heart pounded uncontrollably with excitement.

After pretending to be asleep for about a minute, he just couldn't stand the suspense any longer. He needed to know whether or not he had the new Boro shirt.

Sliding silently out of bed, he watchfully opened his bedroom door and began to tip toe down the stairs wearing his red and white pyjamas. If his mum and dad caught him now, he would be in serious trouble. They had specifically told him to stay in his room until he was called in the morning.

He heard the same sound again, so he stopped, sat on a stair, and waited.

Eerily, the shadowy figure of a man slowly appeared

by the front door. He was clearly getting ready to go out in an old belted brown overcoat, a fawn flat hat, tan leather gloves and a red and white woollen scarf with tassels at each end. Inside the deep pockets of the overcoat he placed a metal tube and a large key.

Jack had seen enough. He quickly concluded that the man was obviously trying to steal the Christmas presents, so he decided to go and wake his mum and dad. As he stood, the stair unexpectedly creaked. The figure instantly turned towards the distraction.

When Jack saw the round, ruddy and radiant face that greeted him, he breathed a huge sigh of relief. The mysterious stranger was his Grandad Charles.

The old gentleman, who had lived with them for the last two years since grandma had passed away, immediately placed his right forefinger to his lips and beckoned Jack to come quietly down the stairs.

As Jack reached the hall, his Grandad was in the front room removing the gold-topped battery from the back of the clock on the mantelpiece. The hands had stopped at one minute to midnight. Jack wondered what on earth his Grandad was up to.

'Go and get your coat from the hall, some warm socks from the tank cupboard and your trainers from the shoe rack in the kitchen,' whispered Grandad, as he hid the battery behind a cheerful wedding photo of Jack's mum and dad, 'there's something extremely important that you must see outside.'

Jack did as he was instructed.

'Surely we're not going fishing at this time of night?' he asked himself. 'Only Inuits and their huskies would dare venture out in this Arctic weather.'

Chapter Two

As they stepped onto the powdery virgin snow Jack lightly held his Grandad's left hand for some reassurance, which was just as well, because he was immediately taken aback to find that all the modern buildings where he lived had been transformed. Union Street was now completely different from his new estate. The houses appeared quite small and they were all joined together in long rows as far as the eye could see.

'All right Charles?' called out a middle-aged man on the opposite side of the street. 'It's a grand night for it.' he suggested, as he pulled his red and white bobble hat over his ears to protect them from the biting cold.

The stiff North Easterly breeze was driving the snow into Jack's face, so he deliberately lowered his head against the cheek-stinging chill. The next time he looked up he realised that the number of pedestrians was growing steadily and they all appeared to be heading purposefully in the same direction.

He also noticed that everybody seemed to recognise his Grandad. They either waved enthusiastically or made a point of saying hello. Jack had not really appreciated that his Grandad was such a popular and well respected person in the neighbourhood.

After walking for only a couple of minutes, Jack became aware of a large queue up ahead, the members of which were all wearing the same outdated clothes and coloured scarves as his Grandad. Some of them even looked like doctors or lab technicians in their decorated long white coats.

'Maybe they're going to a Christmas fancy dress party,' he thought to himself.

As grandfather and shy grandson advanced towards them, the gathering fell reverentially silent. It was just like being in church on Sunday. Nobody said a word.

By now there were so many piercing eyes focussing in on them that Jack felt slightly intimidated, so he gripped his Grandad's left hand for further reassurance.

As they reached the front of the queue they turned sharp left and began to walk down a narrow gloomy alleyway. Nobody followed them. Instead, a mass of inquisitive faces waited behind in the street watching intently as Jack Hartley and his Grandad tentatively approached a set of high red wooden gates.

Grandad took the large key out of his right hand overcoat pocket and as he did so he whispered a strange word, which Jack had never heard before, "Erimus."

Magically, as if it was obeying a command, the key began to glow brightly through the darkness, illuminating the area in which they were standing. Grandad placed the key in the rusty lock and turned. The gates dutifully parted.

As they walked gingerly through the opening, Jack

could see, just ahead, a series of smaller enclosed gates protected by metal barriers.

Grandad Charles hesitated for a moment and looked down at his grandson. His kindly face then broke into the broadest of smiles as he asked, 'Are you ready to go through the turnstile?'

Jack nodded his head in agreement, albeit rather nervously.

Standing authoritatively inside the turnstile, behind an iron grill, was a dapper man with round NHS spectacles precisely balanced on the end of his nose. He was wearing a chequered flat cap, a navy blue double-breasted three-piece suit and around his neck was a red and white woollen scarf tied in a meticulous Windsor knot.

'Now then, can we have a squeeze please?' said Grandad, as he lightly held onto Jack's shoulders.

'Certainly Charles, good to see you once again,' replied the turnstile operator in jocular recognition.

'I'm sure we'll have another memorable night,' he added.

Grandad pushed the metal bar round and they clicked their way through the circular mechanism together.

Almost immediately they were dazzled by an incandescent wall of penetrating white light. It was so intense they had to raise their hands to shield their faces.

Chapter Three

Eventually, once their eyes had become accustomed to the brightness, they moved slowly forwards to a steep concrete stairway with tubular metal handrails on either side. Before Jack began to climb, he glanced back over his right shoulder and observed that the people from the street were now pouring expectantly through the turnstiles.

'Why did they wait for his Grandad to lead the way?' he asked himself. It was turning into a rather strange evening.

When they reached the summit of the concrete steps Jack's mouth dropped open wide in genuine shock and astonishment. The unexpected panoramic view simply took his breath away.

There laid out before him was a traditional football

ground with the most vivid emerald green pitch he had ever seen. The white light flooded down onto the shimmering turf from four huge metal towers in the corners of the ground.

'Welcome to Ayresome Park Jack,' said Grandad Charles with a satisfied smile on his face, as if he was visiting an old friend, 'this is where I used to come and watch my football many years ago.'

Jack had seen various pictures of the famous old stadium in his Grandad's favourite book, Ayresome Park Memories, but he did not expect the real thing to be as grand or as hugely impressive as this.

Opened in 1903, Ayresome Park had been the home of Middlesbrough F.C. until it was closed in 1995. Although over the years it had undergone many structural changes, the ground always remained steeped in local football history and tradition. Countless outstanding players had graced its pristine turf. World Cup matches of 1966, amateur cup finals and England internationals had also been staged there, together with many memorable Boro league and cup-ties.

'Come on Jack, I'll show you around the stadium,' said Grandad zestfully. He was obviously relishing the prospect of being an unofficial tour guide.

They deftly descended down the terracing to where a young man, wearing a black and white St John's Ambulance uniform, politely opened a gate for them that led out onto the small black cinder running track surrounding the immaculate playing surface.

As Jack began to stroll round the pitch, his Grandad Charles waved ebulliently to the exuberant crowd many of whom repeatedly shouted out his name. Jack had never seen his Grandad in such high spirits. He appeared to have acquired a new lease of life since they had arrived inside the ground. His personality had undergone a complete transformation from lethargic senior citizen to passionate football supporter.

Revisiting Ayresome Park evidently meant so much to him.

However, when they reached the renowned Holgate End, Grandad, without warning, suddenly stopped. The reflective look on the old man's furrowed face patently betrayed his personal innermost thoughts. He stared intently at the terracing as he replayed in his mind's eye the years of euphoria and anguish he had experienced standing behind the goal with his friends. The evocative memories of great times all came flooding back: matches, songs, players, goals, promotion, relegation, cup defeats, mates and first girlfriend, they flashed by in an instant, as if it was only yesterday.

'You know Jack,' said Grandad in a soft voice, almost breaking with emotion, 'once you start supporting this club it's in your blood forever, it never leaves you.'

The sincere sentiment was rhetorical. It was a heartfelt outward expression of how very deeply the pensioner felt about his hometown football club, "The

Boro."

Grandad's concentration was ultimately broken by the intervention of a strapping sergeant from the local constabulary.

'Very well done Charles another marvellous occasion!' exclaimed the policemen, shaking Grandad vigorously by the hand, 'what a shame we don't get more of them.'

After exchanging pleasantries, Grandad guided Jack round to The South Stand with its imposing television gantry precariously situated on the sloping roof.

They then moved onto the wide expanse of the East or Bob End, as it was affectionately known because in years gone by it had only cost a shilling to get in. And when Grandad told Jack that a bob was worth five pence he was astounded because today his dad paid at least twenty-five pounds to watch a match.

The old Bob End was once a vast concrete terrace dominated at its centre by a large alphabetical half-time scoreboard. In one corner it also housed the Boy's Enclosure from where Grandad had watched many Boro games. (Well, watched wasn't strictly true, because like most of the lads in the nineteen fifties and sixties Grandad expertly vaulted over the wall and disappeared into the crowd to find his mates, before the solitary policeman on duty could catch him.)

Finally, the conducted tour terminated in front of the North Stand with its unique semi-circular roof, which at one time boasted the longest single advert in the country and the square Longines clock that somehow reassuringly never displayed the correct time.

Chapter Four

As the two tourists sat on a bench near the centre line to snatch a short break, Grandad Charles reached into his pocket and removed the much-travelled metal tube.

'This Thermos flask belonged to my father and it's been to every Boro home game since we won the Division Two championship in 1929,' he announced with pride.

'Not to mention umpteen away fixtures,' he added.

He then twisted one end, removed a cork, and poured hot tomato soup into a cup, before passing the steaming liquid to his grandson. Jack was grateful for the warming drink on such a chilly night.

'Well what do you think about it all?' asked Grandad Charles throwing his arms open wide.

'It's absolutely awesome,' said Jack, utterly

enthralled by the whole colourful spectacle, 'everybody's so happy. But what year is it?'

'It can be any year you want it to be,' said Grandad, much to Jack's surprise.

'Once you're back inside the ground you have the power to relive your own private Boro memories, from absolutely any era. Those memories can be of exciting teams, thrilling league and cup games, inspirational players, fantastic goals or even your very first home match. Many people just come back to meet old friends from years ago with whom they shared some of the happiest times of their lives. I can guarantee that there will be many emotional reunions here tonight.'

As Jack looked around he could see exactly what his Grandad meant. Grown men were excitedly shaking hands and embracing as if they had not seen each other for some considerable time. There also seemed to be plenty of jokes and good-natured wisecracks about being bald, overweight and wearing glasses. It was wonderful to see so many relaxed people in a place where they were utterly content.

As Grandad stood up to put the flask back in his overcoat pocket he looked straight at Jack and said, in a somewhat serious voice,

'Football Jack is extremely important to the people of Teesside. They are very proud of their team. So when these special supporters revisit Ayresome Park it's like a pilgrimage. They are returning to their spiritual football home.'

Grandad could see Jack didn't really understand the emotive significance of what he was trying to say. His words probably sounded like the nostalgic meanderings of an elderly gent who was living in the past. Well, he had heard that accusation before on numerous occasions. However, he strongly believed that future generations of supporters should be made fully aware of the Boro's historical roots and that the club's local heritage and traditions should never be forgotten or deliberately undervalued.

'Come on young Jack it's time to go,' said Grandad, adopting an altogether more cheerful tone, 'I have to meet the players in the dressing rooms.'

'Players. Did you say players Grandad?' Jack asked excitedly, thinking he may have misheard.

'Didn't I tell you,' said Grandad Charles knowingly, as he acknowledged the raised arm of the pipe smoking newspaper reporter wearing a trilby hat in the press box, 'we've come here to watch an exhibition match between "The Boro's" former players who are no longer with us. Reds verus Whites.'

As Jack eagerly followed his Grandad down a narrow tunnel under the stand, a pungent aroma assaulted his nostrils.

'Ugh! Grandad what's that horrible smell,' he shouted in disgust, while holding his nose between the thumb and forefinger of his right hand.

'Oh that, it certainly clears your nasal passages

doesn't it?' laughed Grandad. 'It's called 'Elliman's Embrocation.' The players rub the smooth white liquid onto their legs to prevent pulled muscles.'

Before Grandad Charles opened the door and entered the changing room, he politely asked Jack to wait for him outside. He was planning to arrange something very special for his grandson and didn't want to spoil the surprise.

As Jack stood patiently in the pale light of the corridor, he could overhear snippets of genial banter and raucous laughter as the players, who constantly talked and shouted across each other, jovially recalled their favourite stories and anecdotes.

'What about when you nailed his shoes to the floor?'

'Me? That wasn't me, I cut the legs off his pyjamas bottoms on an away trip.'

'And the time we made the apprentices strip off on a cross country run.'

'No the best stunt was when we drained the boss's

petrol tank dry.'

'Nah, nah, don't agree. Wintergreen in the skipper's jockstrap gets my vote. I seem to remember it certainly warmed him up during training!'

There were howls of hilarity following the last suggestion, but as Jack had no idea about the physical discomfort caused to a player by the application of Wintergreen to his nether regions, the joke rather went over his head.

After about five minutes the changing room door swung open and Grandad Charles reappeared smiling with delight. He then handed Jack an envelope and said advisedly, 'Put this in your coat pocket for safekeeping. Now, we'd better get back to our spec pretty sharpish, they're just about ready to kick-off.'

Chapter Five

Grandad Charles and young Jack hurriedly crunched their way along the cinder track, past the Salvation Army brass band playing, "Old Charlie Take It Away," so they could watch the match in the Holgate End from behind Grandad's favourite barrier, which was halfway up the terrace, just to the left of the goal.

The metallic sounding tannoy "Hustled" into life as the "Gentle" dulcet tones of the Radio Ayresome announcer welcomed everybody to the ground. And when he read out the teams, every former player's name was greeted with huge acclaim.

An air of mounting anticipation began to build until suddenly, there was a deafening fanfare as the opening few bars of a rousing tune called the "Power Game" blasted through the tinny loudspeakers. Jack didn't know why, because he had never heard the music before, but it made the hairs on the back of his neck stand on end.

The players, who were wearing the style of kit from the era in which they played, emerged from the tunnel in the middle of the North Stand to a terrific roar from the capacity crowd. Their warm breath ghosted up into the cold crisp night air. The brilliance of the floodlights vividly highlighted the blood red shirts against the glistening background of the green turf. Jack was totally captivated by the spellbinding drama as it began to unfold.

When the match eventually kicked off, some of the legendary Boro players on view quickly caught Jack's eye. Specifically, a diminutive, golden haired forward, wearing number ten, who dribbled for fun. He was very skilful and clearly enjoyed teasing the other players who could not dispossess him, so good was his close control. Then there was the mercurial number nine in a v-necked red shirt sporting a closely cropped crew cut. He had a shot at goal almost every time he entered the penalty area. Another player to attract his attention was the aptly named "Tiny" goalkeeper in the thick green woollen jumper, who made some superbly agile and athletic saves.

At half time Grandad Charles introduced his grandson to the delights of hot Bovril (or was it Oxo). Jack thought the drink tasted like thin Sunday roast gravy, but it was still very warming.

Standing on a terrace to watch a football match was so different to anything that Jack had ever experienced before. Usually at a modern top-flight game he sat next to his dad. The only occasions they stood up were when the teams came out, and they clapped to the beat of the repetitive music, or when the Boro scored a goal. The rest of the time, like most of the other supporters, they remained seated and relatively quiet.

But here at Ayresome Park it was completely

different. Jack was free to move around, jump up and down and loudly shout out encouragement. There were no florescent orange stewards with wires dangling from their ears repeatedly issuing trivial, self-important instructions. No inconsiderate individuals returning to their seats fifteen minutes after the interval smelling of drink and dropping chips down your back. Jack just loved the carefree atmosphere. He really felt fully involved in the match.

Although the personnel of the teams changed at the break, in order to give as many players as possible a game, the second half was just as exciting.

In particular, one handsome, elegant player with a moustache, wearing number three, seemed to win every tackle he made. He also formed a very solid left sided defensive partnership with the cultured number six in the white-banded red shirt.

Jack then overheard a man, who was standing just in front of them, say that the combative centre forward in the long baggy shorts once scored fifty-nine goals in season. But Jack thought he must have got his numbers wrong because today whole teams didn't even score that many goals.

The extraordinary match was over far too quickly. The final 5-4 score line in favour of "The Reds" was irrelevant. The nostalgic occasion was the real winner.

Before the teams finally left the pitch they congregated in the centre circle and waved their appreciation to the crowd, who in return gave the players a rapturous ovation.

'Did you enjoy that Jack?' asked Grandad Charles. But Jack wasn't really listening. He was savouring the highly charged emotional moment as the fans paid their fitting tribute to "The Boro" heroes of yesteryear.

Grandad could tell however, from the wide-eyed expression on his grandson's face, that it was an experience the lad would remember for the rest of his life.

Chapter Six

'Jack!' The boy glanced over in the direction of his Grandad's gently raised voice, 'wait here for me, while I go and congratulate the players. I'll be back in a few minutes. We have to be the last ones to leave ground so I can lock the gate.'

Jack nodded in acknowledgement and promptly pulled himself up to sit on top of the metal barrier.

From his high vantage point he watched his Grandad walk triumphantly down towards the North Stand, again accepting the plaudits of the crowd as he did so.

Jack wondered why they were still clapping him even though the exhibition match had now finished.

'Your Grandad's done us proud tonight young man,' said a distinguished looking elderly gentleman dressed in an stylish black Crombie coat, as he walked up to

Jack's perch. 'But we might have to wait a long time to see another match.'

'Why?' asked Jack rather puzzled by the negative comment, 'there'll be another game next week'

'Unfortunately not,' said the gentleman in a rather resigned tone, 'it might be years. It all depends on the unpredictable vagaries of the British weather.'

The gentleman could see from the blank look on the boy's face that he was making no sense at all, so he decided to give the lad a more detailed explanation of what he was trying to convey.

'Do you have any idea, young man, who Charles really is?'

'Of course I do,' Jack replied brusquely, in answer to what he considered was a rather daft question, 'he's my Grandad.'

'Well. Yes. But apart from that,' smiled the gentleman at the youngster's very indignant response. 'He's The Ayresome Angel,'

'The Ayresome what?' queried Jack, rather perplexed by the religious pseudonym.

Although the elegant gentleman detected the understandable note of scepticism in Jack's voice, he calmly continued his story anyway.

'Many years ago, some dedicated supporters of Middlesbrough Football Club formed an association called "The Ayresome Angels." They were an extremely loyal group of fans that followed "The Boro" both at home and away.

Through their shared passion for the club many of them became close friends and met regularly to reminisce. A few of the more senior members could even remember games way back to World War One.

When the Ayresome Park ground was closed in 1995, the members were distraught because they thought all their personal football memories would be lost.

Happily however, fate intervened when the association's oldest member and chairman, Sam

Stephenson, attended the stadium's closing down sale.

Sam, who was a lifelong Boro fan, dearly wanted to own an authentic memento from the ground, so he successfully bid for a small office desk.

Once he got it home, he painstakingly began to restore the scratched wooden surfaces.

Then Jack, one day in his workshop Sam made a discovery that would not only change his life, but also that of thousands of other Boro supporters forever.

As he removed one of the shabby drawers, he found a tiny spring-loaded catch. When he pressed it, a hidden compartment slid open in the front of the desk. Inside the compartment Sam found a dusty old brown envelope. He very carefully ran a sharp paper knife along one of the sealed ends and emptied the contents out onto the desktop. The items he found included: a handwritten note, a large key and a unique programme from the first ever league game at Ayresome Park. The note, which was dated September 12th 1903 and commemorated the stadium's official opening, said:

To whom it may concern,

'Please find enclosed, with my compliments, the spare key to the West End of Ayresome Park. The gate can only be opened by the oldest, most trusted, and loyal supporter of Middlesbrough F. C. who knows the true meaning of Erimus.'

Yours sincerely,

Mr. A. Leitch. (Stadium Architect)

'When Ayresome Park was eventually demolished,' the gentleman continued, 'and the new housing estate was built on the stadium site, the only remaining original entrance to the West or Holgate End as it later became known, was down the narrow alleyway.

Every day in the months that followed, Sam Stephenson conscientiously attempted to open the gate, but without any success.

Then Jack, one snowy Christmas Eve, Sam slipped and slithered his way down the icy alley. Once again, as he tried the key in the corroded lock, he distinctly whispered the ancient Latin guiding maxim of Middlesbrough, "Erimus," (We shall be).

To his utter astonishment the gate opened easily.

When he entered the Holgate End through the manned turnstile and eagerly clambered up the stairway, he rediscovered his football heaven. There was floodlit Ayresome Park just as he remembered it, in all its glory, preserved for posterity.

He watched in awe as the legendary players of the past practised their skills on the flawless turf. They all waved at him and the trainer, who wore a large tweed flat cap and had a white towel draped over his shoulder, called out, 'Glad you could join us Sam. What took you so long? Now go and tell all your friends, who love "The Boro" as much as you do, how to find us.'

'And that's exactly what he did Jack. Sam Stephenson

told the dyed-in-the-wool Boro faithful how they could return to Ayresome Park and relive their football memories.'

Jack paused for thought, and then asked rather bluntly, 'But what happens to your memories when you die?'

'A very good question,' acknowledged the gentleman, 'to which there's a very simple answer. It all depends how much you love "The Boro."

If, deep in your heart, you really are a dedicated Boro supporter of a certain age, then your football spirit will automatically be transported right back to Ayresome Park. There it will remain forever alongside all the other spirits you've seen here tonight.'

Jack paused again to try and make some sense of the fantastic tale.

Then he continued, 'But why was my Grandad chosen to receive the key?'

Very impressed by the lad's logical thought process the gentleman explained,

'Well just before he passed away, Sam Stephenson formally handed over possession of the key to your Grandad. By accepting the key, Charles became the oldest surviving Ayresome Angel. The power to unlock the Holgate End and gain access to Ayresome Park was then transferred to him.'

After absorbing the intriguing revelation, Jack was now stunned into total silence.

'What an absolutely amazing story,' he thought to himself. 'If you really loved "The Boro" then your football memories would live on forever. Wow!

And now it was his Grandad who was THE person with the gift of making Ayresome Park memories come true. How cool was that?'

As Grandad came striding resolutely back up the steep terracing, the elderly gentleman gave Jack a buff coloured piece of paper and draped his own red and white woollen scarf around the boy's neck before wishing him a very Happy Christmas.

Chapter Seven

'I'm afraid it's time we went home,' said a breathless Grandad Charles.

Then, placing a reassuring arm across his grandson's shoulders, he asked, 'Where did you get the scarf?'

'From this kind gent…,' Jack stopped abruptly in the middle of his sentence. The elderly gentleman had gone. The ground was now completely empty and silent.

As they half-heartedly plodded their way to the top of the Holgate terracing, Jack put the piece of paper the gentleman had given him in his coat pocket and then turned round for one last, lingering look at the imposing historic stadium.

'So that's what Boro supporters meant by the "good old days." It must have been really brilliant to come here for every game,' Jack thought to himself.

He felt very privileged to have visited the ground, which had played such an important and influential role in shaping "The Boro's" footballing identity.

Ayresome Park was now shrouded in a thickening mist, which was drifting up from the River Tees on the high tide. It created the illusion that the majestic grandstands were beginning to fade away.

Suddenly, Jack was overcome with sadness. It was the sort of feeling you sometimes get when you have to return home after an enjoyable holiday and leave behind newfound friends.

Somehow, deep down, he knew he would never return to this mystical place but at the same time he also knew he would never forget it.

The powerful beams of white light from the four great metallic pylons gradually began to dim as grandad and grandson reluctantly traipsed back to the high red gates.

As Grandad Charles turned the key in the lock to

close the portal, he said a little prayer to himself. He quite selfishly hoped that sometime in the near future it would snow once again on Christmas Eve so he could return to his beloved Ayresome Park, his own spiritual football home.

He placed what was now an ordinary looking key back in his overcoat pocket together with his father's Thermos flask and trudged rather dejectedly back to Union Street with Jack by his side.

It was Christmas Day tomorrow but at this precise moment in time he did not feel the least bit merry. He just felt emotionally drained.

The pavements were now deserted and the snow was beginning to slowly melt away as the temperature rose steadily. All they had for company now was a full moon, which glinted down from the clear night sky.

As they very quietly entered the house, Jack stealthily climbed the stairs to his bedroom while Grandad went straight into the lounge to place the battery back inside the clock. As he did so the suspended hands were released from their slumber and they ticked forward to midnight heralding in the festive season.

Chapter Eight

'Jack, Jack wake up it's nearly nine o'clock,' he heard his mum call out impatiently from the bottom of the stairs, 'I thought you would have been up ages ago to open your presents.'

Jack was tired out. He felt as though he had been up all night. In his crystal clear dream his Grandad Charles had taken him to a Boro match.

As he slid slowly out from under the warm duvet and stretched his arms above his head, he peered through the bedroom window. Even though it was Christmas Day some delivery lorries were still pounding their way across the flyover, the estate was back to normal and there was no snow laying on the pavement. Definitely a dream then, he concluded.

However, as he turned to go downstairs he was

startled to see an old fashioned hand-knitted red and white woollen scarf hanging, rather proudly, over his bedroom door. At one end of the scarf he noticed a small white identification label. He carefully studied the name neatly sewn onto it in red stitching. It said Sam Stephenson. Alarm bells began to resonate very loudly in his head.

Jack instinctively reached over to his coat, which was on the back of the computer chair. Protruding out of the right hand pocket was an envelope and a buff piece of paper. He gently removed them and read out loud the personal writing on the front of the envelope.

To: Jack
Merry Christmas
Up the Boro
Grandad and "The Lads"

Inside the envelope was a folded white document.

Jack very cautiously opened it out. It was rather official looking, with an impressive embossed red letterhead stating: Middlesbrough Football & Athletic Co. Ltd, Ayresome Park, Middlesbrough, Yorkshire.

As he studied the amazing list of autographs written on the page, his hands began to shake in disbelief. It read like a Who's Who of famous Boro players of the past. A real treasure trove of legendary signatures.

He then looked more closely at the buff piece of paper and realised it was a four page match programme.

On the front cover was a detailed black print of the old stadium with the world famous Transporter Bridge in the background. In the centre were numbered lists of the star-studded teams who had played in the match.

He really had been to Ayresome Park. It wasn't just a product of his over fertile imagination.

Jack carefully placed the unique mementoes in the top draw of his bedside table for safekeeping and then bounded energetically downstairs to find his parents and Grandad eating their breakfast in the kitchen.

'Merry Christmas everybody,' he said elatedly.

'Merry Christmas,' they all replied in unison.

'Well hello sleepy head, glad you could join us!' joked his mum, 'we didn't think you were ever going to get up.'

'Were you out at an all night party?' teased his father.

'You could say that dad,' Jack replied truthfully.

He then looked across the kitchen table at his Grandad Charles.

"The Ayresome Angel" winked, smiled affectionately at his young grandson, before continuing to eat his doorstop of a bacon sarnie.

'Now where's that new Boro shirt I was promised?' Jack asked himself as he walked decisively towards the pile of carefully arranged presents under the Christmas tree.

The alleyway is still there.

So let's hope it snows on Christmas Eve.

J.W.